Seriously SILLY stories

Written by Laurence Anholt
Illustrated by Arthur Robins

ORCHARD BOOKS
338 Euston Road, London NW1 3BH
Orchard Books Australia
Level 17/207 Kent Street, Sydney, NSW 2000

First published in Great Britain by Orchard Books: *Little Red Riding Wolf* 1998, *Rumply Crumply Stinky Pin* 1996 and *The Rather Small Turnip* 1996. This bind-up edition first published in 2013.

A Paperback Original

ISBN 978 1 40832 422 6

A CIP catalogue record for this book is available from the British Library.

1 3 5 7 9 10 8 6 4 2

Printed in Great Britain

Orchard Books is a division of Hachette Children's Books, an Hachette UK company.

www.hachette.co.uk

☆ Ghostyshocks ☆ Snow White ☆ Cinderboy ☆ Eco-Wolf ☆
☆ The Greedy Farmer ☆ Billy Beast ☆

LITTLE RED RIDING WOLF

In the very darkest corner of the deep dark wood sat the Big Bad Girl.

The Big Bad Girl was just about as
BIG and BAD as a girl can be, and all
the woodland animals were afraid of her.

She hung about beside the forest path and carved her name on trees. She shouted rude things at any little animal who passed by.

The Big Bad Girl tripped up little deer.
She stole fir cones from baby squirrels and
threw them at the poor little hedgehogs.
The woodland birds didn't dare to sing
when the Big Bad Girl was around!

But the person the Big Bad Girl liked to tease most of all was a charming little wolf cub who often passed by on his way to visit his dear old granny wolf.

Little Wolfie was the sweetest, fluffiest, politest little cub you could ever hope to meet. He would run along the path, *skippety-skip*, carrying a basket of freshly baked goodies for Old Granny Wolf, singing all the time…

"I'm a little wolfie, good and sweet
I am tidy, I am neat.
With a basket full of lovely grub,
I am Granny's favourite cub."

"Wot's in yer basket today, Little-Weedy-Wolfie-Wimp?" snarled the Big Bad Girl. "Mmmm, apple pies? I'll take those. Jam sandwiches? Very tasty."

"Oh dear, oh dear! Now there will be
nothing for dear Old Granny Wolf," wailed
Little Wolfie. And his little wolfie tears
rolled into the empty basket.

Now, the Big Bad Girl's father was not big and bad at all. He was a kind old hat-maker who loved hats in every shape and size, and thought everyone should wear one night and day.

But the sad truth was, his hats were so awful that nobody would buy them. He had only sold one nightcap in his entire life, and the family was terribly poor.

"I can't understand it," he sighed. "I make
these marvellous hats from dawn till dusk
until my fingers are worn to the bone, but
even my own daughter will not wear them.
Please, my dear," he begged, "wear this one
for me."

"Father," answered the appalling child,
"I would rather wear one of your old socks
on my head than this hat. Why can't you get
a decent job? Nobody is a hat-maker these
days. Couldn't you be a woodcutter like
other people's dads?"

The Big Bad Girl hated hats so much that
as soon as her father gave her a new one, she
would run into the woods and give it to a
baby badger or a little squirrel to wear,
whether they liked it or not.

Then, to her father's dismay, she would return home, bare-headed, pretending she had lost the hat in the forest.

One day, however, the Big Bad Girl's father made her a hat that was more ridiculous than anything he had made before. This one was a real monster. It was bright red with a woolly

bobble on top, little flaps over the ears and dangly bows to tie under the chin. It even had a small red cape to match. The old man was delighted with his creation. "Surely my daughter will LOVE this one," he laughed, jumping up and down with excitement.

But the Big Bad Girl said, "Father, you have made some vile things in your life, but this hat is THE PITS! I would rather wear your old underpants on my head. You have as much fashion sense as a dung-beetle!"

As her father lay weeping in his workshop, the Big Bad Girl stomped into the forest to find some unsuspecting little animal to wear the red riding hat.

But, alas, this one was so awful that no
one would touch it. Even the Woodland
Oxfam shop sent her away.

The Big Bad Girl sat by the forest path wondering what to do.

"Surely someone will be stupid enough to wear this hat," she said. As she spoke, she heard a delightful little song…

And who should come along the path,
skippety-skip, but Little Wolfie.

"Ah, ha!" sniggered the Big Bad Girl.
"Here comes Creepy-Cutesy-Custard-Cub.
My red riding hat would suit him perfectly!
I will trick him into wearing it. Then I will
make fun of him FOREVER! Heh heh
heh!"

"Where are you going, Little Fluffy Flea
Face?" growled the Big Bad Girl.

"I am off to visit my darling old granny wolf," replied Little Wolfie, politely.

"Well, I have just seen yer old granny wolf," lied the rotten girl. "You can't see her today because she is poorly and might give you her old granny wolf germs."

"Oh, poor Old Granny Wolf," sighed Little Wolfie, sadly.

"But," continued the wicked girl, "she has made you a lovely sort of hat thing. She told me to give it to you and tell you never to take it off, night or day, even if people laugh at you."

Little Wolfie was very pleased...

…until he saw the revolting red riding hat.
Then even he had doubts.

But being a good little chap and wanting to please his granny, he tied it on his fluffy little head with the dangly ribbons.

The Big Bad Girl almost choked with laughter.

Holy Sweaty Snake Socks! she thought. This little wolf is UNBELIEVABLY stupid.

But Little Red Riding Wolf said 'thank you' politely and set off home, *skippety-skip*, chattering away to himself.

"How pleased I am with my new riding hat that Granny has made me. From now on I will call myself *Little Red Riding Wolf*. That will please her even more."

The Big Bad Girl rolled on the path and roared with laughter. "Holy Newt's Knickers! LITTLE RED RIDING WOLF!! What a name! A wolf should be called *Hairy Howler* or *Bone Cruncher* or *Old Yellow Eyes*. Little Red Riding Wolf is a TERRIBLE name."

All that day, Little Wolfie wore the red riding hat and tried not to notice when people laughed at him.

The next morning he said to himself, "Surely my dear old granny wolf will be better today. I will run along the path and show her how pleased I am with my lovely hat." And off he went, *skippety-skip*...

"I'm a little wolfie, so polite,
I am brave, I am bright,

I am happy, I am good,
In my new red riding hood."

BUT, by the side of the path, in the middle of the deep dark wood, blowing bubbles with her gum, something REALLY NASTY was waiting for him…

"I am not Tomato Head," said Little Red Riding Wolf, fighting back the tears. "I am Little Red Riding Wolf."

"Where are you going, Ketchup Cap?" demanded the Big Bad Girl, wiping her filthy nose on the back of her hand.

"I am going to dear Old Granny Wolf's house to see if she is better and to thank her for this lovely hat. Now, excuse me while I fill my basket with these pretty spring flowers for her kitchen table."

While Little Red Riding Wolf picked his flowers, the Big Bad Girl picked her nose thoughtfully. "That wrinkly Old Granny Wolf will spoil my fun," she said to herself. "I will take a shortcut to her house. If she gives me any trouble, I will lock her in the cupboard, then I will pretend that I am Old Granny Wolf. I bet she is even smaller and weedier than little Strawberry Top."

So the Big Bad Girl ran as quickly as she could to Old Granny Wolf's house. It was a very big house for a little old granny wolf.

But Old Granny Wolf was out chopping
wood in the forest.

43

The Big Bad Girl climbed in the back
window and ran indoors, just as Little Red
Riding Wolf tapped at the door.

"Old Granny Wolf, Old Granny Wolf. It
is I, Little Red Riding Wolf, in my brand
new hat."

"Holy Hopping Hedgehog Droppings!
That was quick," said the Big Bad Girl.
She ran up the stairs and searched for
somewhere to hide. She noticed a huge
bed, but how could she make herself look
like an old granny wolf?

On a hook on the
back of the door,
the Big Bad Girl
found Old
Granny Wolf's
pink lacy
nightcap.
Little Wolfie
had bought
it for Old
Granny Wolf's
birthday, but
she never
really wore it.
Of course, the
Big Bad Girl
HATED hats –
and this one
was even worse than
the red riding hat.

But the Big Bad Girl had no choice. She pulled the ghastly nightcap right down to her eyes and climbed into the bed, just as Little Red Riding Wolf came running up the stairs, *skippety-skip*.

"Old Granny Wolf, Old Granny Wolf. Where are you?" he called.

"Er, over 'ere, Little Woolly Hood Head," answered the Big Bad Girl.

"Oh Old Granny Wolf, Old Granny Wolf, thank you for the beautiful hat you made me. Doesn't it look wonderful?"

"Er…yeah, Little Bobble Brain…really wicked," replied the Big Bad Girl.

"But Old Granny Wolf, Old Granny Wolf, what a tiny voice you have and what small teeth you have too. Perhaps you are still poorly. You seem so pale and weedy today."

"Listen, Little Jam Man. You should learn not to make personal remarks!" snapped the Big Bad Girl.

"But Old Granny Wolf, Old Granny Wolf what small ears you have. In fact...I don't think you are my old granny wolf at all. She is MUCH bigger than you."

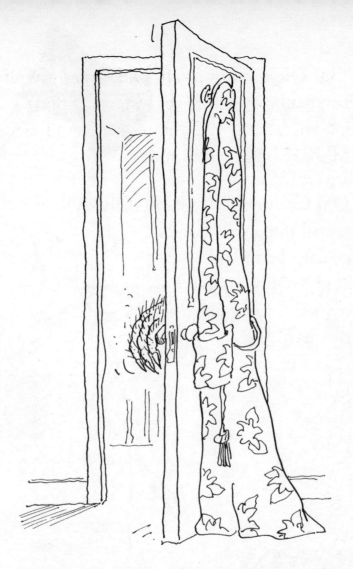

At that precise moment Old Granny Wolf
pushed open the door...

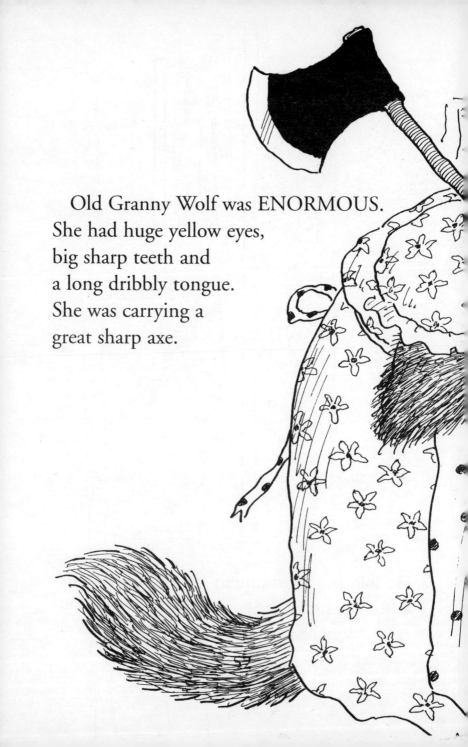

Old Granny Wolf was ENORMOUS.
She had huge yellow eyes,
big sharp teeth and
a long dribbly tongue.
She was carrying a
great sharp axe.

"Ah, Little Wolfie," she said. "What a nice surprise. You are just in time for tea. But why are you wearing that ridiculous hat? And what is this thing in my bed? It looks like a Big Bad Girl – a very tasty Big Bad Girl – just right for my BIG BAD TEA!"

The Big Bad Girl leapt out of bed, down
the stairs, out of the door, into the forest
and along the path as fast as her big bad legs
would carry her. She hammered on her
father's door.

"Father, Father," yelled the Big Bad Girl. "Let me in. Let me in. I will be good. I will do whatever you ask."

Her father peeped out of the window. He couldn't believe what he was seeing. There was his daughter wearing a delightful nightcap. It reminded him of one he had made himself many years before... He remembered it well because it was the only one he had ever sold.

"I will let you in," he said. "But only if you promise to wear a hat night and day – the one you are wearing now suits you beautifully!"

And so from that day on, the Big Bad Girl became a Big Good Girl (for most of the time). She found a job as a woodcutter, and her boss kept a very careful, big yellow eye on her.

The Big Good Girl kept her promise to
wear a hat every day, although it was usually
a chainsaw helmet.

And the red riding hat was useful…

...when they had an especially heavy load.

RUMPLY CRUMPLY STINKY PIN

There was once a country where everyone
had silly names.

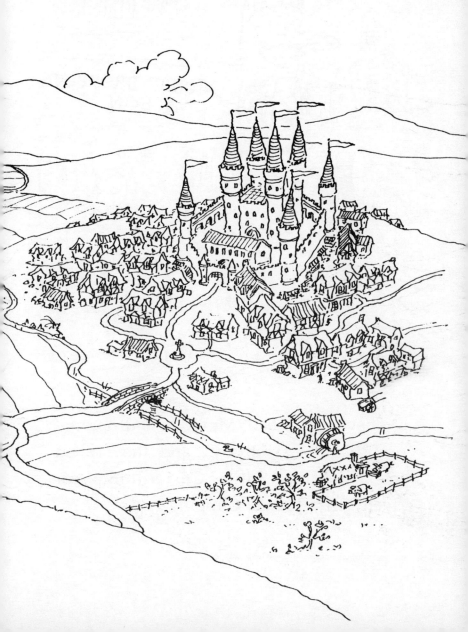

They were called 'Mrs Mouse-dropping'
or 'Roland Camelbelly', and they called
their children 'Little Custardlump' or
'Teeny-Tiny Toenail Clipping'.

But the person with the silliest name of all was the king himself and he was very proud of it.

His full title was 'His Royal Niceness
Marvin Eggbeard Pyjamadance Birdwhistle
Gormangeek Bob-a-job Kneepickle Burp
Glub-glub Globba Blobin Eeeeee Woomph
Paint-Your-Mother-Green – Junior III'.
Which is a pretty good name for a king.

Now, in this country lived a miller by the name of Eyebrow Snailsocks. Eyebrow had a beautiful daughter who he was always boasting about, "Not only is she beautiful," he would say, "but she is clever too."

My daughter can do ANYTHING! Why, I bet she could...I bet she could...make string vests out of spaghetti!"

"Don't be silly, Daddy," the girl would say. And everyone who knew old Eyebrow only laughed.

But one day, the king (whose name I have mentioned) heard of Eyebrow's idle boasts. "Send your daughter to me," he ordered, "let's see how clever she really is."

The miller was very frightened and his daughter began to shake and weep into her apron, but the king's order had to be obeyed.

Before she left, Eyebrow promised to buy his daughter anything she wanted to make up for the trouble his boasting had caused.

His daughter couldn't think of anything offhand except perhaps a little fluffy guinea pig for a pet. And this Eyebrow promised her as soon as she returned from the palace. (Assuming she was still wearing her head.)

And so it was that the young girl stood shaking before the king.

"DO YOU KNOW WHO I AM?" he demanded in a deep royal voice.

"Yes sir," whispered the girl. "You are 'His Royal Niceness Marvin Eggbeard Pyjamadance Birdwhistle Gormangeek Bob-a-job Kneepickle Burp Glub-glub Globba Blobin Eeeeee Woomph Paint-Your Mother-Green – Junior III'."

"Exactly," said the king. "Now, your father has been boasting that you can knit string vests out of spaghetti. I have decided to lock you in a room full of spaghetti and if it isn't all knitted into string vests by sunrise, I will personally tickle your armpits with a wet toothbrush."

Saying this, the king swept out of the
room and went off to practise signing his
name.

The miller's daughter was in despair, she looked at the mountain of spaghetti and thought of the little fluffy guinea pig she would never see. Then she wept into her apron again.

All of a sudden she heard a funny little laugh:

Tee hee hee hee !

And looking down at her feet she saw the strangest little man she had ever seen. He wore a pointy hat and had an orange beard which was so long that he had wrapped it three times around his waist.

"I know," she sobbed. "I have to knit all this spaghetti into string vests otherwise the king will tickle my armpits with a wet toothbrush."

"Oh please help me," sobbed the girl.

The little fellow grabbed an armful of spaghetti and pulled two enormous knitting needles from his pocket. But suddenly, he paused, and looked up at the girl

The poor girl searched her apron pocket which was soaked with tears and finally pulled out a soggy toffee which the little man seized with delight.

The girl danced with joy as vest after vest
flew from the flashing needles.

CLICKETY CLICK!
We'll make
these vests
in a tick.

Early in the morning the king brought
the miller to watch the toothbrush tickling.

Of course, he couldn't believe his eyes when he unlocked the door and saw that every last bit of spaghetti had been made into perfect little string vests, all with tomato buttons down the front, as neat as you please.

"What did I tell you?" boasted Eyebrow Snailsocks (pretending not to be surprised) "I said she was clever. My daughter can do ANYTHING! Why, I bet...I bet she could make bank notes out of OLD FISH."

"Oh Daddy!" groaned the miller's daughter. But it was too late, the king was already ordering a room to be filled to the ceiling with old fish.

"Right!" he shouted. "If she fails I'll…
let's see…I'll plant melon seeds between
her toes and…if she succeeds then…I'll
marry her."

Well, the miller's daughter didn't much
fancy having melon seeds planted between
her toes…

…but, on the other hand, she didn't like the idea of being married to the king either; especially if she was going to be called 'Her Royal Niceness Marvin Eggbeard Pyjamadance Birdwhistle Gormangeek Bob-a-job etc etc'.

As soon as she was alone with the mountain of fish she began to weep into her apron. Surely no one could make bank notes out of old fish? Now she was sure she would never have the fluffy guinea pig her father had promised her.

Suddenly the room was filled with strange laughter . . .

. . . and the little man stood before her again, singing in his squeaky voice.

The girl told the little man about her
father's boasting and the king's order that
she should make bank notes out of old fish.

She was just getting to the bit about the melon seeds, when the little man pulled a printing press from his pocket and began throwing the fish in one end and pulling crisp new bank notes from the other, singing as he worked . . .

"Anything, anything," promised the poor girl, frantically searching her apron pockets. But alas! There was nothing there.

The girl gladly agreed and by sunrise not one minnow remained. The room was stacked to the ceiling with neatly folded, slightly smelly bank notes.

"Let's marry immediately!" shouted the king throwing open the door.

Eyebrow jumped up and down with delight. "You see!" he yelled "I told you she was clever. This girl can do ANYTHING! Why I bet . . . . I bet . . ."

But the miller's daughter was gone,
down the stairs and out of the palace.

Later, as he walked home, the miller began to feel very sorry about all the porky pies he had been telling, and all the trouble he had caused.

So remembering his promise, he called in
at the pet shop and bought his daughter the
cutest, fluffiest little guinea pig he could find.

The girl was delighted and soon forgot about the horrid king and the strange little man. But that night as she lay in her bed listening to her new pet running round and round on his squeaky wheel, she heard someone laughing outside her door. . .

The girl didn't wear her apron in bed, so she wept into her pyjamas instead. "Don't take my guinea pig," she pleaded.

The little man felt sorry for her and said. . .

In a flash, he was gone. The girl lay awake
for the rest of the night thinking of likely
names for him.

The next evening, the little man returned.

But the plucky girl was determined to try. "Is it Scrambled Egg Foot?" she asked. But the little man only laughed. . .

Tee hee hee hee!

. . . and stroked his long orange beard.

"Is it Plum-Plum-Lemon-Moose Carpet Ears?" she asked hopefully.

The little man laughed even more.

"Well then, perhaps it's Hubert Crumpet Trumpet-Bum?" the miller's daughter asked desperately.

The little man screeched with laughter and in a flash, he was gone, leaving the poor girl more miserable than ever.

The old miller didn't like to see his daughter unhappy, so at breakfast he told her a story to cheer her up.

"I was delivering flour yesterday when I saw the funniest thing; there was a little man wearing a string vest made of spaghetti, dancing outside a tiny caravan and he was singing the most peculiar song."

"Can you remember the song?" asked the girl, her eyes lighting up.

"Well, yes," said her father. He cleared his throat and sang:

I sing and dance a little jig,
Soon I'll have that guinea pig.
They can weep a bowl of tears.
They won't guess my name
in a billion years.

"It did make me laugh I can tell you!"

"Yes, yes, but didn't he mention HIS NAME?" shouted the girl.

"Whose name, my dear?" asked the puzzled miller.

"THE LITTLE MAN, you old toad!" snapped the girl.

"Oh no," said the miller, "he didn't."

The poor girl began to despair and a big tear ran down her pale cheek and into her boiled egg.

"Don't cry," said her father, "I can tell you his name – it was painted on the side of his caravan: Rumply Crumply Stinky Pin. Magician. (Spaghetti Vests A Speciality)."

"That's it," cried the girl clapping her
hands with joy.

That night, as she was feeding her guinea pig, the little man appeared again.

Come on kid, have you given up yet? Don't waste your time, just hand me the pet.

"I'll just try again," said the clever girl. "I might be lucky this time. Is it Benny Badger-Brain or Eddy Earwax-Eater?"

The little man rolled with laughter.

"Perhaps it's Trevor Telephone Bone Helicopter-Head!"

The little man was lying on the bed, kicking his legs in the air.

"I'll have one last try," said the miller's daughter, "and the guinea pig is yours. Is it . . . RUMPLY CRUMPLY STINKY PIN?"

The little man almost choked with rage
and vanished in a clap of thunder, filling
the air with a strange smell of burning
spaghetti and old fish.

So, the miller's daughter lived happily ever after with her guinea pig and her old father, who hardly ever told lies any more.

"What will you call your little pet?" asked Eyebrow Snailsocks one day. "How about Guinea-Winnie-Winkie-Wigs or Pinkie-Poky-Porky-Piggy Pants?"

127

"Oh no Daddy," said the girl. "I think I'll just call him . . . Fred."

"That is a *very* silly name," said Eyebrow Snailsocks.

And it was.

Moral: A guinea pig is for life, not just for Christmas.

THE RATHER
SMALL TURNIP

Round about lunch time, the greedy farmer began to feel hungry. His huge belly rumbled as he walked across the field.

Suddenly, he noticed a rather small
turnip. . .   .

134

. . . but it was far too small for his lunch.

The farmer called over to his wife.

"Here you are, wife," he said, "you can have this nice turnip for your lunch."

The farmer's wife looked at the rather small turnip. She poked it with her boot.

"You mean old thing!" she said to her husband, "I won't get very fat on that!"

So the farmer's wife called the cow.

The cow looked at the turnip.

She poked it with her hoof.

"There you are," said the farmer and the farmer's wife, "we're feeling generous today. You can have this delicious turnip all for yourself."

145

"You must be joking," mooed the cow, "that's not enough for a big girl like me. Call the goat."

The goat looked at the rather small turnip.

He prodded it with his horn.

149

"We have chosen this beautiful turnip especially for you," said the farmer and the farmer's wife and the cow. "Would you like to eat it here or take it away?"

"You must be kidding," bleated the goat. "I've never seen such a lousy specimen. Give it to the dog."

The dog sniffed the turnip.

"Go on," said the farmer, his wife, the cow and the goat. "Tuck in."

"Don't make me laugh," barked the dog.
"I don't even like turnip. Call the cat."

The cat came. . . slowly.

"Guess what?" said the farmer, the farmer's wife, the cow, the goat and the dog. "It's your lucky day. You can have this turnip boiled, mashed, poached or steamed – all garnished with side salad and served with house wine."

159

"Humph!" miaowed the cat, looking at the turnip. "I've got bigger blisters than this turnip. Send for the mouse."

The mouse scampered across the field.

163

She came to the place where the farmer,
the farmer's wife, the cow, the goat, the
dog and the cat were standing.

At their feet
was the most
beautiful turnip
she had ever seen.

The mouse stared and her pink nose twitched. She couldn't believe her luck. She LOVED turnips.

She sniffed it. She licked it all over and her eyes sparkled.

"Don't wait for us," said the farmer, the farmer's wife, the cow, the goat, the dog and the cat.

169

So the tiny mouse began to eat. She nibbled and gnawed.

It took a long time because, to her it was a very BIG turnip.

The others watched and waited and felt more and more hungry. The greedy farmer's belly rumbled.

The mouse crunched. . .

. . . and scrunched.

And chewed. . .

. . . and chomped.

Until, at last, every scrap of the rather small turnip was gone.

Then the tiny mouse burped a tiny burp,
sighed a tiny sigh, rubbed her tiny fat
mousy tummy. . .

. . . and lay down in the grass for a tiny
mousy sleep.

The cat looked at the fat little mouse.

"Now. that's what I call LUNCH!" she growled. And she gobbled up the little mouse in one bite.

Then. . . the cat was eaten by the dog. . .

. . . the dog was eaten by the goat . . .

184

. . . the goat was eaten by the cow . . .

... the cow was eaten by the farmer's wife ...

187

... and the farmer's wife was eaten by...

"WAIT A MINUTE!" shouted the farmer's wife, "You can't eat ME!"

"But what about my lunch," moaned the greedy farmer.

"Well," said the farmer's wife, patting her tummy. "You should have eaten that turnip. It was absolutely delicious!"

Billy Bonkers

'Utterly bonkers!
A riot of fun! I loved it!'
– Harry Enfield

**Mad stuff happens with Billy Bonkers!
Whether he's flying through the air propelled
by porridge power, or blasting headfirst into a
chocolate-covered planet – life is never boring
with Billy, it's BONKERS!**

**Three hilarious stories in one from an award-
winning author and illustrator team.**

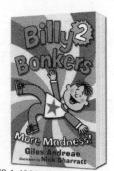

978 1 84616 151 3 £4.99 pbk

978 1 40830 357 3 £5.99 pbk

978 1 40831 465 4 £4.99 pbk

ORCHARD BOOKS

www.orchardbooks.co.uk

Max and Molly's Guide To Trouble!

Meet Max and Molly: terrorising the neighbourhood really extremely politely...

Max and Molly's guides guarantee brilliantly funny mayhem and mischief as we learn how to be a genius, catch a criminal, build an abominable snowman and stop a Viking invasion!

978 1 40830 519 5 £4.99 Pbk
978 1 40831 572 9 eBook

978 1 40830 520 1 £4.99 Pbk
978 1 40831 573 6 eBook

978 1 40830 521 8 £4.99 Pbk
978 1 408 31574 3 eBook

978 1 40830 522 5 £4.99 Pbk
978 1 408 31575 0 eBook

ORCHARD BOOKS

www.orchardbooks.co.uk